It Will Take a Lot of Us
To Lift a Hippopotamus

RT

Ringtail Learning
San Francisco

It Will Take a Lot of Us
to Lift a Hippopotamus

Copyright 2013
Hans and Jennifer Hartvickson
Printed in the United States of America
First Edition

Published by
Ringtail Learning
San Francisco, CA

ISBN: 978-0-9828866-4-9

Library of Congress Control Number: 2012919556

For order information, visit misterlemur.com

A portion of profits from this book will be donated to charities supporting the protection of lemurs and/or lemur habitat.

Manufactured by Thomson-Shore, Dexter, MI (USA); RMA586MS244, November, 2012

To parents...

...and everyone else who
pulls together.

I've never heard so many yips
and squawks and urgent grunts.
Each voice was yelling different things,
and they all yelled at once.

The sound was quite cacophonous,
a big bombastic din.
I tried to listen to them all,
but where could I begin?

cacophonous: having a harsh, unpleasant sound
bombastic: having a loud and inflated style
din: a loud and continued noise

2

The alpha lion roared, "Enough!"
And silence quickly fell
on the crowd that had assembled
'round the edge of Old Stone Well.

alpha lion: the lion with the highest rank in a group

3

"We do not have much time to spare.
By now you all have heard
that a younger hippopotamus
has wandered from his herd.

"We think that he was being chased,
but we can't really tell.
Regardless how it all went down—
he's fallen in the well.

"This will not be an easy task,
but still, it must be done.
This hippo's name is Kubu
and he must weigh half a ton.

"Come forward now and state your case.
This is your chance to say
why you're uniquely qualified
to come and save the day."

Two elephants then raised their trunks.
One loudly spoke the boast,
"Of all who live inside this park,
we clearly lift the most."

This pair of pachyderms was strong,
and there was little doubt
that they had the needed size and strength
to pull young Kubu out.

Impalas cheered. The warthog yelled.
And those who had hands clapped…

7

...but Kubu did not budge at all.
Instead the rope just snapped.

8

A buffalo approached the
well and mumbled he supposed
that he'd thought of one solution
that no one had yet proposed.

"This plan may sound impossible,
but I'm prepared to try.
Please lower me into the well.
I'm going to drink it dry."

The gathered mass discussed his plan.
They found it lion-hearted,
but most unlikely to succeed.
The plan was never started.

lion-hearted: brave, courageous

Then one hyena made a joke.
He just could not refrain.
He said, "Why don't we lift him out
with Storkly – he's a CRANE!"

11

The largest brains inside the park
belonged to chimpanzees,
who thought themselves to have the smarts
of tenured Ph.D.s.

"We are much smarter than you all.
Ergo, our contribution
will be to tell you simpletons
the one correct solution.

tenured Ph.D.: an experienced teacher with an
advanced academic degree suggesting high intelligence
ergo: therefore

"We cannot extricate him now.
He's far too tightly stuck.
So clearly we must lubricate
the walls with goop and muck.

"And once his arms and legs are loose,
he'll have the range of motion
to simply climb out by himself
and end this whole commotion."

extricate: to free from an entanglement or difficulty

The chimps then made a formula
they called "Chimpanzee Paste,"
a mix of mud and sand and leaves
and some chimpanzee waste.

They made 200 gallons and
they poured it in the well.
We crossed our fingers it would work,
then tried to block the smell.

A somber silence then ensued.
Time passed. We grew concerned.
Two birds flew in. Two birds flew out.
They told us what they'd learned.

"Our little flight into the well
allowed us to surmise
that the mud's displacing water
and the water's on the rise.

---

surmise: to form an opinion based on incomplete evidence
displacing: to take the place of a liquid, causing the
level of the liquid to rise

"And Kubu still can't free himself,
we'll need to save him soon.
It looks like it's eleven now.
We think we have 'til noon."

The lion then walked toward our group,
and with an agile leap,
he bounded spryly to the hood
of our safari Jeep.

The lion seemed so gentle that
I barely could refrain
from reaching out to touch his face
and stroke his regal mane.

---

agile: quick and well-coordinated movement
spryly: nimbly
regal: fit for a king or queen

"Despite heroic efforts from
our strongest and most clever,
we still cannot get Kubu free.
I fear we may not ever!

"And now we're running out of time.
We don't know what to do.
We don't know who to ask for help,
and so... we're asking you."

I thought for a few moments,
then I slowly raised my hand.
I said, "There are some valid points
to each scheme that was planned.

"But each of these plans on its own
has done more harm than good.
You have not tried combining them,
and I think that you should.

"No one can do this task alone.
It seems to me that, rather,
we'll have to do this as a team
and lift him out together!"

The lion roared a mighty roar
to signal he agreed,
and then he roared instructions for
the things that we would need.

Those with thumbs repaired the rope.
Some gathered more supplies.
A crew jumped in a mixing pit
of swimming pool size.

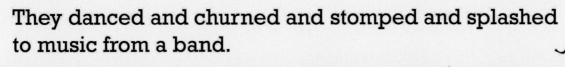

They danced and churned and stomped and splashed
to music from a band.

The lion roared to tell the team,
"The moment is at hand!"

The air was thick with urgency
and drama and suspense.
The pulling team braced for the pull,
their muscles strong and tense.

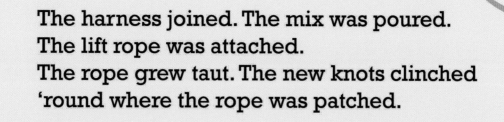

The harness joined. The mix was poured.
The lift rope was attached.
The rope grew taut. The new knots clinched
'round where the rope was patched.

taut: tightly stretched

24

Together they were oh-so strong
(and Kubu oh-so slick)
that the final lift-out from the well
was painless and was quick.

He tumbled right out of the well
onto the muddy ground.
He stared in stunned amazement at
the crowd that gathered round.

He stammered in the mid-day sun,
"I never was aware
that I had so many awesome friends
who really seem to care!"

stammer: to say something in a hesitant way

26

We took a photo as a team,
then went along our way.
I promised I'd come back to see
the friends I made that day.

27

I opened up my journal then
and made a little note.
I did not know where to begin,
and so, I simply wrote,

"It sure did take a lot of us
to lift that hippopotamus."

ABOUT THE AUTHORS

Hans Hartvickson has been writing stories and poems since he was in first grade. He loves sharing the fun of rhyming stories with kids of all ages.

Hans holds a bachelor's degree in Economics from Stanford University and an M.B.A. from The University of Pennsylvania's Wharton School.

A ring-tailed lemur whispers a story idea to Hans

Jen Hartvickson travels the country speaking to schools, art associations and after school programs about the importance of writing, setting goals and making plans.

Jen earned a bachelor's degree in Sociology and a master's degree in Education from Stanford University.

Jen shares her love of writing with students

Other books and albums from Mister Lemur and friends:

You can find all these and more on my site, misterlemur.com

Jen performs a handstand on the rim of the Ngorongoro Crater in Tanzania while a local Maasai herdsman stands guard.

Cool facts I learned:

The word "kubu" (pronounced "KOO boo") means "hippopotamus" in Lozi, an African Bantu language spoken in Zambia, Zimbabwe, Namibia, Botswana and parts of South Africa.

It Will Take a Lot of Us to Lift a Hippopotamus is set in the Ngorongoro (pronounced "ong-GORE ong-GO-row") Crater in Tanzania.

While the majority of the animal species depicted in this book live in the Ngorongoro Crater, chimpanzees and giraffes do not. They have been included in this book due to their contributions to the story.

I went on this adventure with my friends (and bandmates):

my sister

Jenny Hart

Silky

Numbat

Lemur Pup

Kori Bustard

Impalas

Flamingos

Crowned Crane

Wildebeest

Hyenas

African Buffalo

Warthog

Mister Lemur